A DIMASH QUDAIBERGEN FABLE:
THE SCULPTOR'S MASTERPIECE

Pamela McGee Wilkinson

A DIMASH QUDAIBERGEN FABLE:
THE SCULPTOR'S MASTERPIECE
Copyright © 2022 by Pamela McGee Wilkinson

All rights reserved. No part of this publication may be reproduced, distributed, or transmitted in any form or by any means, including photocopying, recording, or other electronic or mechanical methods, without the prior written permission of the publisher or author, except in the case of brief quotations embodied in critical reviews and other noncommercial uses permitted by copyright law.

ISBN: (Paperback)   978-1-63945-433-4
        (Hardback)   978-1-63945-434-1

The views expressed in this book are solely those of the author and do not necessarily reflect the views of the publisher, and the publisher hereby disclaims any responsibility for them.

Writers' Branding
1800-608-6550
www.writersbranding.com
orders@writersbranding.com

Contents

Preface v
Dedication ix
Introduction xi

The Sculptor 1
The Sculptor's Masterpiece 8
The Masterpiece Is Real 19
Mr. Qudaibergen and Me 29

PREFACE

If you purchased this book out of curiosity and you do not REALLY KNOW WHO DIMASH QUDAIBERGEN IS YET, then this preface could serve as a foundation for your interest in him. I hope.

EVERYTHING that I present to you is based on knowledge and information I have collected over the last three and a half years since my discovery of his talent. And most of this information came from his televised interviews over the years. My journey with him and his music is no different than millions of other fans or Dears as he refers to us. We belong to a unique fandom that is built on a mutual admiration for his God-Given-Talent and his character. Any serious Dear could write their own book about Dimash.

Dimash says he cannot remember a time when he wasn't interested in music, performing and being on a stage. Around the age of three he was leaping from his grandmother's lap to run to the stage and take bows with his performing parents. I'm sure the audiences lapped it up. As soon as he could handle a tape player on his own, he was going to bed with it and listening as long as he could until sleep overcame him. I'm just guessing here but that might have been the bedrock of his four to five hours of sleep a night to this day.

By the time he was age five and going to school, he was already adamant that he wanted to take music classes, vocal and instrumental, along with regular required studies. For years, his paternal grandmother saw to that by taking him to his music school every school-day morning for three hours: a great sacrifice on her part that Dimash to this day announces to the world and he appreciates it more than he can say.

And at that age he was pitch perfect and could sing to his music teacher each note she chose on the piano. At six he won first place in a piano contest with his peers. That was just the beginning of first-place certificates, plaques and trophies and of course, some nice money prizes along the way, which he said was deposited into his creative center's account to help support his career. Dozens and dozens of first places for singing awarded from his country, and neighboring others, began an inevitable consequence of recognition.

In the winter months of 2016, after receiving an invitation and then accepting it from a very popular Chinese singing contest, Dimash became famous in China overnight when the first episode of the months-long contest was televised in January of 2017. He was watched and admired by hundreds of millions of new fans for subsequent episodes and Dimash now entered the entertainment world that he had aspired to perhaps a decade earlier. A notable insert here should include that he was competing with established well-known singers from China. He was the first foreigner to be invited and at age 22 was the youngest to ever compete in the yearly contest. He lost first place for the first time EVER, but only by a fraction of a point. Neither Dimash nor his millions of new fans cared about the photo-finish results.

China was the beginning in an international sense and eventually Dimash will be singing in North and South America often and other countries around the world he has yet to set foot on. He continues to grow his fan base thanks to his YouTube channel and his social Internet sites and millions of Dears who spread the word and attempt to convert more Dears.

What makes him so special or unique? His vocal range!!! Remember when he was five and could sing back to his teacher with pitch-perfect perfection each key she stroked? Well, now imagine twenty-three years of vocal lessons that could take up three hours of his time each day. I have yet to hear Dimash admit to his vocal range limits. Maybe he has no limits and he is too humble to admit it or it's one of the many things about which his family will not allow him to boast. We're happy to boast at least seven octaves for him and a handful of semi-tones. Add to that a lung capacity, that very few have, that is capable of delivering a belt, and most often with liquid-like vibrato, for up to 25 seconds. Add to that, his desire to create an unearthly world while he sings to you. His stage presence gets scores of 100 from vocal coaches. They say he is doing everything right when it comes to emoting and pulling you into his songs and his world. It works! EVERYTIME!!!!

Add to that, (yes I'm still adding and I hope you're keeping up) the fact that his CONFIDENCE when he steps on any stage is phenomenal. He oozes it and we hope he never, ever "loozes" it!!! Then add to that, his gratitude and appreciation at the end of his performances that he tries to convey to the audiences. I say he tries because he recently declared that "Words cannot convey how I feel about and love my Dears". Many of those sitting in the audiences have travelled a dozen hours or more by plane to be a listener. Others have travelled far distances by car, bus or train. His fans for his concerts can represent up to sixty countries - very impressive for any singer/performer.

His character/persona today was built on a foundation of attentive and loving grandparents and parents who supported him in every way imaginable. Their sacrifices helped him build a career that will soon be known worldwide. They did not just support his desire to be a great singer/performer but they also spent years, mostly by example, teaching and encouraging him to be a good citizen and patriot of his homeland, Kazakhstan. They taught him about his country's ancestors who sacrificed even their own lives to make their country special, safe and independent. He sings songs about them in every concert. He adds to his concerts some samples of his instrumental abilities also, especially the dombra. We love that thing. He features well-known Kazakh virtuosos of various instruments in his concerts and guest appearances. This singer and instrumentalist is not above supporting and encouraging others' talents.

He is an angel, an alien, an android created by musically gifted scientists and some DNA from his parents. And simply put, an incredible phenomenon of singing. He teaches us all that music has no national boundaries. And we have learned that songs can affect us tremendously even if we do not understand the 13 or so languages he uses to convey the lyrics of a song. He IS music to his Dears. He is trilingual (Kazakh, Russian and English) and even his speaking voice is music to our ears and he needs to own that.

Every human being should hear this singer at least once and it's up to them if they want to hear him again and again and again. Every human being deserves air to breathe, food and water, clothing, shelter and someone to love and to be loved….. But as a new dear said recently, "What have I done to deserve Dimash Qudaibergen in my life?" A good question….that may not have an answer for all of us.

Pamela McGee Wilkinson
5 June 2022

THIS BOOK IS DEDICATED TO:

DIMASH QUDAIBERGEN

THE SCULPTOR'S MASTERPIECE

AND OUR MAESTRO OF MUSIC

INTRODUCTION

According to a dictionary I perused, a _fable_ is: A fictitious narrative or statement: such as a legendary story of supernatural happenings.

That definition works for what you are about to read. Some of you have read the first two parts if you purchased my first book, I Am Music – My Journey with Dimash Kudaibergen- The Best Singer in the World. But….it obviously needed more. For my own personal reasons, I have added at the end of each Part, the date that "chapter" was created.

The Sculptor series, if you will, began on December 10th, 2020 after I read some comments from Dears on a fan page I follow. I can't remember the Dears' posts but the comments were something to this effect: "Seriously, where did Dimash come from?" "He's from another planet." "He's not human."

Those kind of comments were nothing new to me, his other fans or Dimash on December 10, 2020 as I've/we've all said them and heard them hundreds of times before but on this particular day, I suddenly thought that maybe he wasn't human after all but was created in an ethereal way and the vision of a Sculptor working on a clay creation of Dimash was planted in my head. I saw the details of his studio and I saw a finished sculpture of Dimash.

If for some reason you purchased this book and are not already a fan (Dear) of Dimash Qudaibergen, please read about him on Wikipedia, find him on all of his social pages and get to know him and by all means discover his songs on his YouTube channel. Except for the seven ancient and modern wonders of the world, we have very few phenomena.

Pamela McGee Wilkinson

THE SCULPTOR
PART ONE

I'll bet that you are special
I am too….so I've been told
But Dimash Qudaibergen? Well, let me tell you
He broke that "special" mold.

The following is a fable
Of how he came to be
For when he was created
He was different than you and me.

For, to create means "to organize"
You begin with thoughts and ideas
and then you add materials
and see what the end result is.

The Sculptor in this creation story
Dreamed a vision late one eve
And quickly tumbled out of bed
To roll up his Sculptor's sleeve.

He examined his usual shelves of molds
that he used almost every day
But scratched his head and grit his teeth
and said "Geez! There's just no way!"

(Now, let's hear the Sculptor's story in his own words)

The vision of that man I saw
Should not come from these average molds
For these are rather common and plain
If the truth be really told.

I wondered while looking up
There are some special molds up there.
Some I've never ever used before
And some I'd never ever share.

I'll have to grab my ladder
for that shelf is way too high
I'm glad I've never used these molds
For now I think I know why.

You see, I bought them long ago
from a man who was sublime
At crafting molds of faces and hands
and bodies of every kind.

I remember now that he told me
that I'm buying the only set
That when and if I use them
That I'm never ever to forget

That he'd never had a vision
or a model that would suffice
To use these molds for just any creation
Because they're really, really nice.

"I'm not trying to be boastful, he said
About my talent or my skill
I'm just trying to convey this thought to you
Before you settle the bill.

That these molds could one day be priceless
Or you may have to throw them away
After you create Your Creation
That's all I am trying to say."

So I paid the gentleman what I owed
And stored the molds away
And said "For now, I'm thinking
I'll just put them on display."

(So the Sculptor went to work that day
With these molds he dusted off
And when he saw what he had created
He stammered and choked and coughed.)

What have I created now?!
Is this really the vision I saw?
Look at those eyes and those perfect lips
That nose....that majestic jaw.

Those hands and fingers look so strong
I know they'll serve him well
He will use them for many, many wonderful things
But for what I could never tell.

What is this art I've created?
He's such a beautiful sight.
His visage is simply ethereal
And how about that height?

He's standing 6 foot 3 inches tall
That's taller than me, and my brothers
His shoulders are wide. His waist is small.
He's just not like all the others.

I'm glad I gave him raven hair
And lots of it to boot
And when it is combed and styled just right
He'll look handsome in any suit.

But something else is going on
He's more than a figure with hair
There's something shining from his face
That makes we want to stare.

It's as if a passion for the spice of life
Is screaming to come out
I'll bet he will be an artist of some sort
Yes. That's what that's all about.

But at the same time when you see his face
There's a light that you will find
There's the power of love and compassion
For all of humankind.

Oh my goodness! What was I sculpting?
This truly is surreal.
I've never created something like him
He's so powerful but so very still.

The glow from his face is almost haunting
His essence is so very strong
He's really not meant to be on this earth
But that's where he belongs.

Who knows what this man will become
If he makes all the right choices
And follows a more than average path
And listens to all the right voices.

I seem to sense his human nature
It's not typical by any means
The world will be aware of that
In full view …and behind the scenes.

Wait! I'm speaking of him as if he is real
This creation made of clay
Why? How are these thoughts coming to me?
Just what am I trying to say?

So now I have these molds to consider
Should I destroy them or put them away
Or should I sell them to the highest bidder
And just go about my day.

No. I'll never ever use them again
And no, they won't be sold
Because this man I've created today
Deserves his own special molds.

Oh, he will set out to conquer the world
And his heart will be on display
And your first look at this earthly Prince
Will be an unforgettable day.

Pamela McGee Wilkinson
10 December 2020

THE SCULPTOR'S MASTERPIECE
PART TWO

(Our Sculptor continued to stare and stare
At this man he had created.
He was captivated by his very essence
He was visibly elated.)

(He paced and paced in his studio.
He tossed his glasses and exclaimed.)
Will someone please tell me what's going on?!
Is there someone out there to blame?

I've never had this feeling before
That I was not the creator.
I feel I'm just the conduit
For something, someone surely greater.

I don't remember when I started
I barely remember the finish.
Was I actually physically here all along?
Oh My! Now I'm just sounding foolish.

Of course I was here and very present.
I remember the hours I spent.
I remember the clay staining my hands
And I remember the feel and the scent.

But my hands seemed to move on their own
As if I had no command.
They shaped. They formed. They fashioned.
They knew how to make this man.

It was practically abnormal and dreamlike
The smell and the feel and the texture.
Was the clay as unusual as the molds?
Or is that just my conjecture?

Do I now understand what the crafter meant
When he said these molds are special?
He even used the "priceless" word
As if he meant "consequential".

I'm having confusing feelings now
To explain these moments in time
When I worked today in this studio
And entered the world of sublime.

So here I stand perplexed as can be.
The answers aren't coming forth.
But there is one thing that is certain to me.
This man has SIGNIFICANT WORTH!

As of now he's just a statue of clay
That happens to be surreal.
I ceremoniously put the molds away
But what is this mystical feel?

(The Sculptor entered his music room
He was bewildered and overcome.
He knew not what to do with this man
But he surmised what he could become.)

I have to take a much-needed break
This mystery is getting to me.
I need a beautiful but simple distraction
But what could that distraction be?

Oh yes! I'll play some classical music
Like Beethoven, Stravinsky or Bach.
(He contemplated which composer to choose
While removing his sculptor's smock.)

I believe a sonata from Beethoven
Would certainly rest my heart.
I'll play the album that I just bought
That sounds like an excellent start.

(He prepared a tea with some honey and lemon
And sat down in his favorite chair.
He closed his eyes and leaned way back
As the music filled the air.

He quickly but gracefully fell asleep
Then his teacup crashed to the floor.
He awakened and thought to clean it up
But sleep....he wanted more.

He settled again into a sweet, sweet slumber
He needed the rest you see
For having a part of the creation that day
Made him tired and drained and weary.

As he napped and entered a dreamlike state
The music's volume seemed to grow.
He didn't make a move at first
But he surely wanted to know.)

Why IS the music getting louder?
Is the player beginning to fail?
(He finally opened his eyes a bit
And noticed a handsome male.)

(He was tall and perfect in his suit.
His presence filled the space.
The Sculptor rubbed his eyes three times
Then recognized his face.)

You're my creation! he said aloud
But you've surely come to life!
What made this happen? Why are you here?
I must go get my wife!

No! Please don't do that. I'll explain.
You can tell her another time.
I am the creation that you helped form
And my form is in its prime.

When you purchased and stored those special molds
It was me that you actually bought.
The crafter was trying to explain it to you
But you couldn't read his thoughts.

He never tried to form me
As he knew it couldn't be done.
He needed a very special artist
And he knew that you were the one.

Oh, there were attempts to buy my molds.
There were others who wanted to try.
But he kindly and politely sent them away
Until you came...by and by.

But what you and I can't explain
And may never really understand.
Is that I was waiting for this very day
To be formed by your skillful hands.

Your human traits, your artistic talent
Was just the help I required
To become the man I've become right now
And I'm so glad you were hired.

But why, oh why are you standing here
And saying all of these things?
What made you come to life at all
And become a human being?

I heard some sounds coming from this room.
They penetrated my heart and my soul.
And then I started to breathe and move
And I found I had complete control.

I stepped quite carefully toward the music.
I wanted to hear more and more.
I saw you were sleeping peacefully
When I peeked through a crack in the door.

I needed to get to those heavenly sounds.
As I neared the player, it knew
That I needed the music to get louder and louder
But I'm sorry it awakened you.

The tones and chords of that sonata, well
It's as if they were speaking to me.
It's as if I was here for this very moment
To discover what I should be.

I know now that musical notes, musical sounds
Will be everything to me.
It will be my desire and my devotion in life
And soon everyone will see.

Before you finally awakened
I stood here for quite some time.
I carefully studied the music I heard
And the notes and tones seemed to rhyme.

I have to be a part of this world.
I know this is where I belong.
I must learn to compose these things
And I must be a singer of songs.

(The Sculptor completely agreed with him
As his passion simply filled the room.
Now he knew he'd created a Masterpiece
And he was watching the Masterpiece bloom.

But he would never fulfill his dreams right here
In the old Sculptor's music room
He would have to leave to find his dream
And he knew it would be very soon.)

So when you're ready and your heart tells you so
Just leave whenever you wish.
You'll know when the time is perfect and right
But first let me tell you this.

You'll live for all of the moments
You can sing the composers' songs.
You'll relish the adoration of family and fans
The world is where you belong.

Musical themes will appear as in dreams
Then the music will pulse through your veins
You'll be found sharing your music to crowds
In halls and in many domains.

Choose smartly and wisely along the way.
Choose friends that will have your back.
Your parents and family will give their support
And help with the things you may lack.

You'll be amazed at the love you'll receive
And not just for your heavenly singing.
But for the humble person you'll become
And because of the love you'll be bringing.

(The Masterpiece thanked the Sculptor
For the confidence he portrayed.
And asked if he could rest a while
Before his departure was made.)

Of course, please rest right here on this couch.
I'll take my comfortable place.
Sleep well and have some pleasant dreams.
You'll have some decisions to face.

(These kindred souls now rested a bit.
It had been an interesting day.
He'd created a singular Masterpiece
From some molds that had been on display.

The hours passed and the sun shone through
The windows to his right.
But the Sculptor found as he opened his eyes
That the Masterpiece was nowhere in sight.

He quickly checked the studio
He even went outside.
He asked his wife if she'd seen someone
And she very smartly replied.)

There's been no one here except you and me
I've been by your side all along.
The illness you have been battling with
Has allowed you to sleep for too long.

You never saw a nice looking man
That stood about six foot three?
You're saying I've been asleep all the while
Please tell me you're kidding me.

Honey, maybe you should go back to sleep.
You're clearly not ready to wake.
If you think there's been a gentleman here
Then it has surely been your mistake.

But please go look at the studio.
You'll see where I used my tools.
You'll see the remnants of clay all around
And my glasses are still on the stool.

But Dear, I'm sorry to tell you this
But the studio looks just fine.
And your glasses are resting on your nose
Unless I am going blind.

Well, perhaps it was a dream, I guess
But as vivid as it could be.
I know this Masterpiece exists somewhere
And how wondrous he will be.

I know you won't ever believe this
Since you think I've been seeing things.
But when that man appears to the world
It's because of the songs he will sing.

His voice will be astonishing.
The people will claim, "He's the best"!
And he'll be a bringer of love and peace
And will tower above the rest.

What a marvelous, marvelous dream to have
And if this man really does exist.
I'm telling you dear when you hear him sing
You'll feel like your soul's been kissed.

I still want to believe he was here for a day
And formed from clay I could feel.
I'm telling you honey. I'm telling you now.
<u>That the Masterpiece is real.</u>

Pamela McGee Wilkinson
January 4, 2021

THE MASTERPIECE IS REAL
PART THREE

(The Sculptor knew his Masterpiece left
On a quest to pursue his art
He wondered how he would fulfill his dream
And wondered how he would start.

As the Sculptor recovered from his long malaise
And returned to his daily grind
He began to sculpt again and again
And was grateful for the use of his time.

But inside of his heart and in the back of his mind
The Sculptor still felt confused
That these thoughts of creating a magnificent man
Could not easily be removed.

These thoughts were with him during the days
And they were with him when he laid down for bed
His wife tried to placate his imagination
But at every chance, she said.)

Darling, does it really make any sense at all
That you spent from an eve to the next eve
Sculpting a man of six foot three
It's so hard for me to believe.

The last time you sculpted the figure of a man
That was measured at five foot nine
It took you a month and a half to finish
I know.... as I recorded your time.

Dreams can be vivid as we all know
They can seem as they really took place
Then our hearts and minds let go of the dream
But for you this is not the case.

I'm so sorry that this is perplexing you
And it's become this obsessive thing
That you created a tall man of clay
Who is destined to compose and to sing.

Please, let's pretend that this never occurred
And get on with our lives as before
You have real sculptures to shape and create
And you have clients that you just can't ignore.

Yes, yes honey. I know you are right
I have to let go of this thing
It's ridiculous and utterly insane to think
That I made a sculpture that will sing.

Thanks for your counsel and your patience
I'll pursue my work as before
Just leave me be in my studio
as I have other things to explore.

(The days and weeks and months rolled by
The couple was happy and peaceful
The Sculptor forgot about his Masterpiece
And went about thoughts that were needful.

Two decades and several years passed
And added to the ages of the pair
The old man retired from sculpting
and the wife made the meals they would share.

He spent his leisure hours reading
and listening to music for his mind
As we know he loved the classics
But now he searched for artists of all kinds.

His tastes were becoming eclectic
He enjoyed opera, jazz and some pop
And once he discovered a brand new genre
From a man who rose to the top.

He sang every note that was on a piano
And his performances were so profound
Our Sculptor started to wonder a bit
Was he the best singer around?

He started to research the singer's beginnings
He was fascinated with his humble speech
He focused on his musical prowess
And all the notes he could reach.

He began to think the singer resembled
Maybe a face from a distant time
But his memory did sometimes fail him
As his aging started to climb.

He spent hours listening to interviews
But the Sculptor was nearly aghast
When one day this artist shared with the world
A special moment from his childhood past.)

" While living in my parents' home
And I was young...about five or so
The sounds of a masterful composer's sonata
Was playing on the radio.

The tones and chords of that sonata, well
It's as if they were speaking to me
It's as if I was there for that very moment
To discover what I should be.

I knew then that musical notes, musical sounds
Would be everything to me
It will be my desire and my devotion in life
And soon everyone will see.

I have to be a part of this mystical world
I know this is where I belong
I have to learn to write these things
I must be a singer of songs."

(The Sculptor leapt from his comfortable chair
He could not believe what he just heard
For nearly 30 years ago in that very room
The Masterpiece had uttered those words.

He remembered he told the Masterpiece
The music will pulse through your veins
You'll be found sharing your music to the world
In halls and in many domains.

You'll live for all of the moments
You can sing the composers' songs
You'll relish the adoration of family and fans
The world IS where you belong.)

So the Masterpiece is very real
and is traveling to all nations.
He is sharing his music to millions of fans
And receiving grand adorations.

Then I did not create this man out of clay
It's ridiculous to think that I did
He was born in the most ordinary way
and grew up as somebody's kid.

He found his passion when he was a child
This precocious Kazakh Prince
Then introduced his "genre specific"
In his concerts and other events.

I'm still perplexed why I had the dream
Why I predicted this Music Man
But I'll support his dream of being the best
If that is this singer's plan.

What a wonderful satisfaction and relief
I can only say how I feel
That even though I did not create him
I'm so glad the Masterpiece is real.

(A matter of days went by so fast
And the Sculptor continued to listen
To song after song of the Masterpiece
But he felt that something was missing.

He was drawn to visit his old studio
That had been closed for business, a decade
And wanted to refresh his memory once again
Of a promise he just remembered he'd made.

There was a certain set of molds he bought
That he used only but once
But he couldn't remember the crafter's name
Or the year of the purchase or the month.

He remembered he stored them high above
On a shelf that he rarely used
He climbed up carefully on his old wooden ladder
That looked unsteady and slightly abused.

He noticed that certain set of molds up there
That he promised he'd never sell or share
And pulled them down for a better view
And tried to take great care.

He turned them over and over again
He was surprised they were in such good shape
But he noticed a piece of paper in a hand
That was fastened with blue painter's tape.

He carefully unfolded the paper in his hands
And read the words that were there...
"Thank you for sculpting me, kind sir
and for being a sculptor who cared.

I'm thankful for the words we exchanged
I'm grateful and blessed that we met
You really are a sculptor of note
And you're someone I will never forget.

When the crafter completed the last of my molds
He stored me in a special place
Years later... just when you walked in
He recognized your face.

He said as he crafted my hands and my throat
That he saw a vision of you
That with heavenly help from an ethereal being
You would bring my life into view.

For I was "born" through your very skilled hands
On the 24th of May '94
You were "guided" to mold and shape my form
And this had never happened before.

You couldn't understand the motions
Your hands were using to create
My body, my face, even my throat
And how they were taking shape.

But soon you will discover me by chance
And see that I'm a singer of songs
I already know my ultimate fate
And stages are where I belong.

They will be my second home
I will feel quite natural on a stage
I'll give my listeners my very best
Then I'll have the listeners engaged.

So thank you once again, my friend
I'm grateful from the heart I was given
To have been created and formed by you
A man who was focused and driven.

By the time you have read this note
I will have pursued the singer's art
My motivation and my determination
Will start from my human heart.

You once called me your Masterpiece
And you said you watched me bloom
I'm humbled that you shared that title with me
When I stood in your music room.

*But I am just an ordinary man
Who just happens to sing for a living
I've been blessed by God to have some talent
And I'm blessed by His penchant for giving.*

*Maybe now you know my name and my story
You did your homework I'm sure
You've found yourself that life can be hard
And good music can be a cure.*

*Continue to develop your human traits
I wish you a wonderful life
I'll give you a wink from a distant stage
Please share this with your wonderful wife."*

The Sculptor could not believe it
The note was officially signed
By the singer that he had discovered
As he searched for new artists online.

He signed the note KDimash
With a tribute to his Dears right below
But how did he guess that nomenclature
So many many years ago?)

So here I am perplexed again
Like I was those years before
Did I make this man out of clay I could feel?
But for now, I don't care to explore.

I'm just so grateful I discovered him
His songs make me feel so alive
And I don't know when this note got here
But I am so glad it arrived.

I feel as if I'm on a journey with him
I'll watch him closely through the years
And join with all the millions of fans
Who call themselves his Dears.

PAMELA MCGEE WILKINSON
March 16, 2021

MR. QUDAIBERGEN AND ME
PART FOUR

(As his retirement would have it
There was plenty of time for leisure
There was plenty of time to inform his friends
Of his favorite singing treasure.

There were a few obsessive Dears
That the Sculptor converted quite soon
But a particular friend he knew in L.A.
Gave him some awesome news that June.

"I have an inside scoop about Dimash
He will soon be singing in Vegas
My wife and I are going for sure
If you want to go, please tell us.

Because of my job as a talent promoter
I've received advanced tickets for four
They include tickets for a meet-and-greet
Which is a concept I'm sure you'll adore."

(The Sculptor was literally laughing and screaming
When he got this good friend's call
He jumped up and down like he was on springs
He even bumped into a wall.)

Of course we will go! We will meet you there
Wild horses couldn't keep us away
But before we're done with this conversation
I really have something to say.

Ken, you are making this old man's dream
Of seeing my favorite star
Come true in the most surprising way
This news is quite bizarre!

For now I will promise you this
That this Sculptor will re-open his place
And sculpt for you anything you want
That has arms and legs and a face.

"That's fine. Just fine, my friend
But a payback is not what I'm after
I just knew you would be thrilled to hear this
And I can tell by your screams and your laughter.

I'll be in touch in a couple of months
And there's something else I'll say
The singer's date to perform in Vegas
Will be on your 75th birthday!"

(Well, that was it! The Sculptor was fried.
He continued to express his emotions
He hoped he could soon tell his favorite singer
The extent of his years-long devotion.

The months crawled by so very slow
Like molasses from a ten-year-old bottle
He filled the time with distracting things
Even read eight-hundred-page novels.

Then the much-anticipated day arrived
It was time to board the plane
His wife begged him to nap on the trip
Or he'd surely drive her insane.

The Sculptor took the nap she petitioned
He was rested when the plane touched down
And now he was seriously wondering
If his feet would touch the ground.

The venue was bright and colorful
They had never been to Vegas before
They promised if they survived the concert
They'd take some time to explore.

The seats the promoter found for them
Were only four rows from the venue's stage
He could tell by the very close distance
He would see every move Dimash made.

For his singing….though clearly phenomenal
Wasn't the only thing he cared to absorb
For his very impressive stage presence
Brought him and so many fans aboard.

Song after song after every amazing song
Dimash delivered with sheer perfection
He felt the Dears' sincere support
And he absorbed their unique affection.

Some favorite songs were sung that night
The Sculptor was physically elated
His wife was clearly a Dear all night
Their enjoyment could not be overstated.

They finally took a moment to breathe
And to think of what they just saw
A sadness came over the Sculptor
But was replaced with wonder and awe.)

"How does he do that this singer of songs
His control and power are sublime
How does his throat cooperate like that?
He sang for more than two hours' time.

Oh, these are questions that I'll never answer
It's up to the experts again
But my gosh, we still have these backstage passes
And now it's time to call Ken.

(They all connected and met outside
In the hallway for meet-and-greets
The line was forming and he would be last
He could actually hear his heart beat.

Dimash exited his dressing room door
There were many other lucky Dears
Who had a chance to meet the Prince
They'd been following for so many years.

He gracefully greeted each star-struck Dear
As if he'd known them forever
He smiled, he laughed, he hugged, nearly cried
Uttered words that were gracious and clever.

He apologized several times to the Dears
that his team was ready to go
He wished he had time for more pictures with them
But he wanted the Dears to know.

That he wouldn't be where he is today
Without their love and support
He was sorry to say there's so little time
And he'd have to keep this meeting short.

He reached out to shake the hand of our Sculptor
But the Sculptor couldn't resist
He pulled Dimash in for a gentleman's hug
By gently pulling his wrist.

They embraced for just a few seconds
Dimash thanked him for attending the show
But then he stood looking very perplexed
And our singer just had to know.)

"Have we ever met before, sir
At another meet-and-greet?
I feel I have stood somewhere with you
And we were standing almost feet to feet."

(The Sculptor began to tell Dimash
That they met many, many years before
In a dream that he had on the singer's "birth" day
As they stood on his music room's floor.)

We talked a lot about your future career
That you would compose and sing
And travel around the whole entire world
And oh, the joy you would bring.

"Wow! You had this dream on the day of my birth?
I saw those things with you too?
And now you're standing here three decades later
I'm so glad that your dream came true.

Well, I have to go now.
I'm so glad that we had the time to meet
I'd love to hear more about your dream
But maybe at another meet-and-greet."

(Dimash was whisked away so quickly
To a car that was waiting on the street
But Dimash didn't leave without hugging his wife
And planting a kiss on her cheek.

Now the couple was completely satisfied
So many dreams of theirs had been met
But now it was time to retire to the hotel
And see how much sleep they could get.

The lavender scent from the silky pillows
Calmed their hearts and minds just fine
And the silky sheets the hotel used
Were apparently the finest kind.

The Sculptor fell asleep in a couple of minutes
And then he started to dream
That he and Dimash were visiting again
In his music room… it seemed.

They talked again of his singing career
And his travels around the earth
He remembered the singer told him back then
That he was the cause of his birth.

The Masterpiece even made a prediction
that maybe one day they'd meet
At one of the singer's concerts
And they'd be standing feet to feet.)

"Won't that be an awesome moment
if we meet again in due time
And we could easily recognize each other
At a future concert of mine?"

(Once again, the Sculptor was puzzled
He forgot the Masterpiece said
That they could meet again in the future
As he dreamed in his hotel bed

He quickly sat up and thought for a second
What that prediction really meant
Was Dimash, HIS MASTERPIECE, once and for all
But now his brain was spent.

For he decided a long, long time ago
That he couldn't sculpt a thing that could sing
And even tried to forget his creation
And think about other things.

But Dimash did say he looked familiar
And let there be no mistake
That our Sculptor really spent some time with Dimash
In a thirty-year-old dream he can't shake.)

THE END

PAMELA MCGEE WILKINSON
MARCH 29, 2021

www.ingramcontent.com/pod-product-compliance
Lightning Source LLC
LaVergne TN
LVHW070046070526
838200LV00028B/404